Farley Found It!

Bruce Van Patter

BOYDS MILLS PRESS

HONESDALE, PENNSYLVANIA

To Will, Nathan, Todd, and Grace,
who make our house a happy home
—B.V. P.

Text and illustrations copyright © 2006 by Bruce Van Patter

Boyds Mills Press, Inc.
A Highlights Company
815 Church Street
Honesdale, Pennsylvania 18431
Printed in China

Library of Congress Cataloging-in-Publication Data

Van Patter, Bruce.
Farley found it / by Bruce Van Patter. — 1st ed.
p. cm.
Summary: When Farley the sheep decides that a cozy doghouse is a
better place to sleep than a scary meadow at night, Edna the dog
must move her house day after day, hoping that Farley will not find it again.
ISBN-13: 978-1-59078-351-1 (hardcover : alk. paper)
[1. Doghouses—Fiction. 2. Sheep—Fiction. 3. Dogs—Fiction.
4. Sleep—Fiction.]   I. Title.
PZ7.V346Far 2006
[E]—dc22
2005037559

First edition, 2006
The text of this book is set in 16-point Rockwell.
The illustrations are done digitally.
Visit our Web site at www.boydsmillspress.com

10 9 8 7 6 5 4 3 2 1

Farley loved his meadow when the dandelions glowed in the sunshine.

But the dark of the night scared him. He didn't sleep well under the stars.

Down by the barn, Edna loved her doghouse and its cozy closeness.

Even when she left for meals, she couldn't wait to get back.

She had a place to call her very own . . .

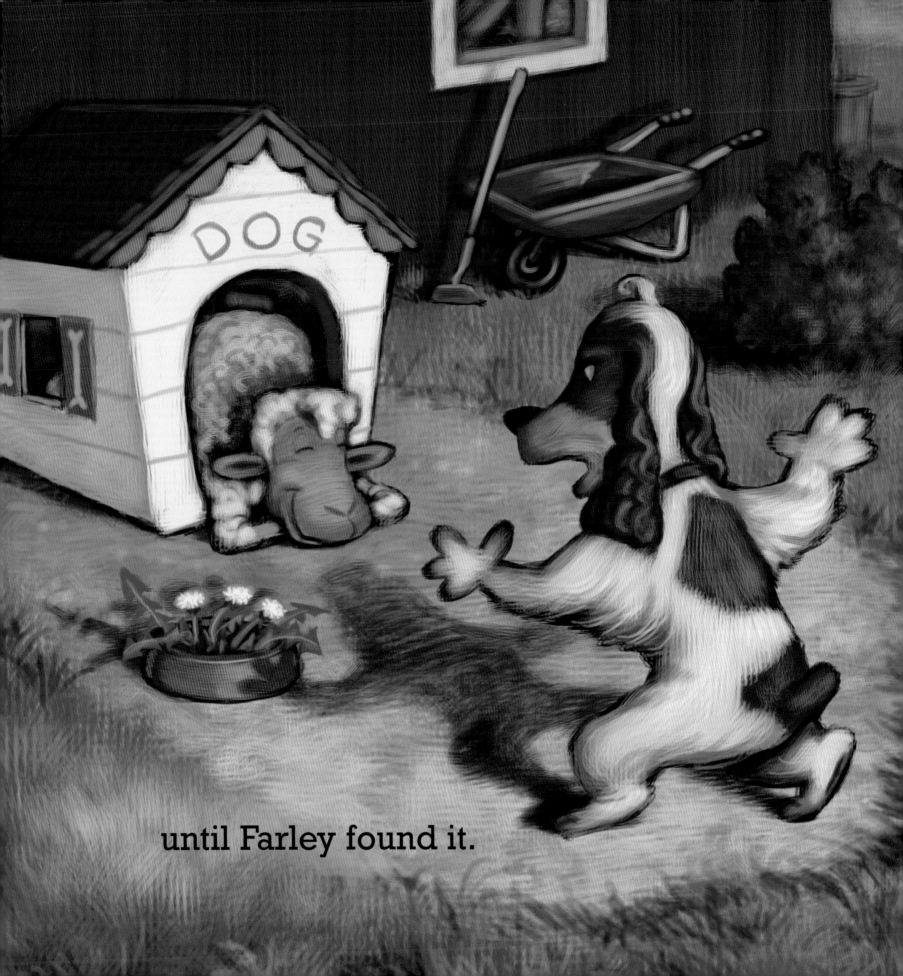

until Farley found it.

"This won't do," thought Edna. She tried to wake him,
but the sheep was having deep, warm, woolly dreams.
For the very first time, Farley slept well.

Edna didn't.

The next day, when Farley went back to his meadow,
Edna moved her house. She searched for a place to hide it.

"He'll never think to look here," she thought as she went for dinner.

But . . .

Farley found it.
He was having soft, rich, velvety dreams.

Edna hid her house in the hay. "A perfect spot," thought Edna.

But . . .

Farley found it.

He was having sweet,
fragrant, grassy dreams.

Then Edna tried hiding it under the henhouse.

But . . .

Farley found it.

He was having snug,
fluttering, feathery dreams.

She even put it high in the great oak.

But . . .

Farley found it.

This time he had green,
breezy, leafy dreams.

At last, the poor dog could take no more.

The next morning, she decided there was only one way to end all the trouble.

And so, there was house enough for both—

at least for a little while.